PowerKids Readers:

The Bilingual Library of the United States of America™

Bilingual Edition
English/Spanish
Edición bilingüe

VIRGINIA

JENNIFER WAY

TRADUCCIÓN AL ESPAÑOL: MARÍA CRISTINA BRUSCA

The Rosen Publishing Group's
PowerKids Press™ & **Editorial Buenas Letras**™
New York

Published in 2006 by The Rosen Publishing Group, Inc.
29 East 21st Street, New York, NY 10010

First Edition

Photo Credits: Cover © Raymond Gehman/National Geographic/Getty Images; p. 5 © Joe Sohm/The Image Works; p. 7 © 2002 GeoAtlas; pp. 9, 31 (hilly) © Walter Bibikow/National Geographic/Getty Images; p. 11 © Getty Images; pp. 13, 15, 25, 30 (Capital), 31 (Fitzgerald, Lewis, Clark, Jefferson) © Bettmann/Corbis; p. 17 © Burstein Collection/Corbis; pp. 19, 31 (festival) Sid Bolden - bluegrassuniverse.com; p. 21 © Medford Taylor/National Geographic/Getty Images; pp. 23, 31 (old-fashioned) © Lee Snider/Photo Images/Corbis; p. 30 (Flowering dogwood) © Raymond Gehman/Corbis; p. 30 (Dogwood) © Owen Franken/Corbis; p. 30 (Cardinal) © Gary W. Carter/Corbis; p. 31 (Washington, Madison) © Geoffrey Clements/Corbis.

Library of Congress Cataloging-in-Publication Data

Way, Jennifer.
Virginia / Jennifer Way ; traducción al español, María Cristina Brusca.— 1st ed.
    p. cm. — (The bilingual library of the United States of America)
Includes bibliographical references and index.
ISBN 1-4042-3112-9 (library binding)
1. Virginia—Juvenile literature. I. Title. II. Series.
F226.3.W3918 2006
975.5—dc22
                                                                        2005028581

Manufactured in the United States of America

Due to the changing nature of Internet links, Editorial Buenas Letras has developed an online list of Web sites related to the subject of this book. This site is updated regularly. Please use this link to access the list:

http://www.buenasletraslinks.com/ls/virginia

Contents

Contenido

Welcome to Virginia

These are the flag and seal of the state of Virginia. Virginia is a state that is proud of its history. Eight American presidents have come from this state.

Bienvenidos a Virginia

Estos son la bandera y el escudo de Virginia. Virginia es un estado orgulloso de su historia. Ocho presidentes estadounidenses son originarios de este estado.

Virginia Flag and State Seal

Bandera y escudo del estado de Virginia

Virginia Geography

Virginia is in the southern part of the United States. Virginia borders Washington, D.C., North Carolina, Kentucky, Maryland, West Virginia, and Tennessee. Virginia also borders the Atlantic Ocean.

Geografía de Virginia

Virginia está en el sur de los Estados Unidos. Virginia linda con Washington, D.C., Carolina del Norte, Kentucky, Maryland, Virginia Occidental y Tennessee. Virginia también linda con el océano Atlántico.

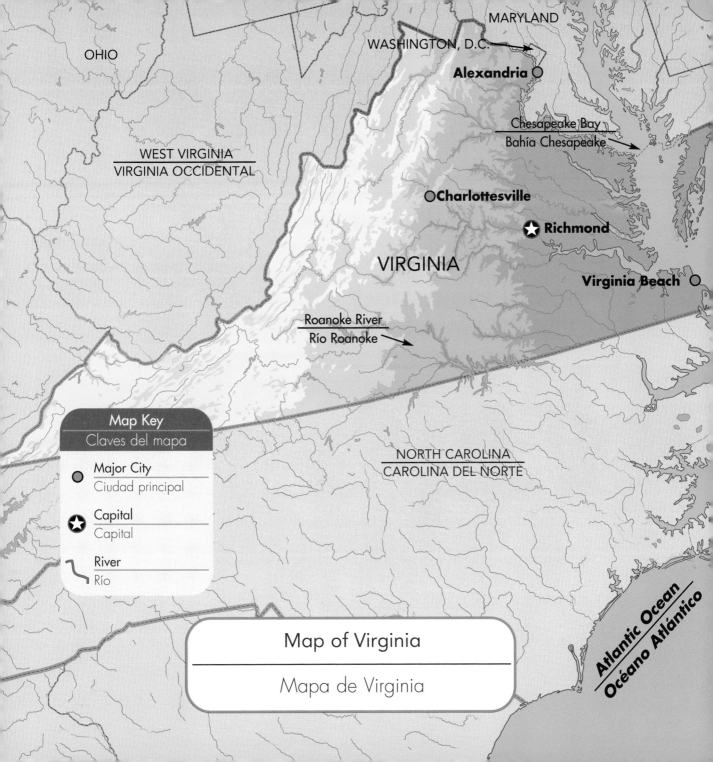

OHIO

MARYLAND

WASHINGTON, D.C.

Alexandria ○

WEST VIRGINIA
VIRGINIA OCCIDENTAL

Chesapeake Bay
Bahía Chesapeake

○**Charlottesville**

☆ **Richmond**

VIRGINIA

Virginia Beach ○

Roanoke River
Río Roanoke

NORTH CAROLINA
CAROLINA DEL NORTE

Atlantic Ocean
Océano Atlántico

Map Key
Claves del mapa

○ Major City
Ciudad principal

☆ Capital
Capital

River
Río

Map of Virginia

Mapa de Virginia

The Blue Ridge Mountains are in the western part of Virginia. Central Virginia is called the Piedmont. This is a hilly area. Eastern Virginia is called the Coastal Plain, and it is low and flat.

Las montañas Blue Ridge están en la parte occidental de Virginia. La región central de Virginia, llamada el Piedmont, es montañosa. La zona oriental de Virginia es conocida como la Llanura Costera, y es baja y llana.

The Blue Ridge Mountains

Montañas Blue Ridge

Virginia History

Jamestown, Virginia, was the first English settlement in the United States that lasted. Jamestown was started in 1607. It was named for James I, who was England's king at the time.

Historia de Virginia

Jamestown, Virginia fue la primera población inglesa permanente de los Estados Unidos. Jamestown fue fundada en 1607 y nombrada en honor a James I, rey de Inglaterra.

Jamestown, Virginia, in 1610

Jamestown, Virginia en 1610

George Washington was born in 1732 in Virginia. He led the Continental army against the British in the American Revolution. Washington became the first president of the United States in 1789.

George Washington nació en Virginia, en 1732. Washington comandó el ejército Continental en contra de los británicos durante la Guerra de Independencia. En 1789, Washington llegó a ser el primer presidente de los Estados Unidos.

George Washington

The Civil War was fought from 1861 until 1865. It ended at Appomattox Court House, Virginia. On April 9, 1865, Confederate general Robert E. Lee and Union general Ulysses S. Grant agreed to end the war.

La Guerra Civil se peleó de 1861 a 1865 y terminó en Appomattox Court House, Virginia. El 9 de abril de 1865, el general de la Confederación Robert E. Lee y el general de la Unión Ulysses S. Grant acordaron terminar la guerra.

Generals Lee and Grant at Appomattox Court House

Los generales Lee y Grant en Appomattox Court House

The first, third, fourth, and fifth presidents of the United States came from Virginia. These presidents were George Washington, Thomas Jefferson, James Madison, and James Monroe.

El primer, el tercer, el cuarto y el quinto presidente de los Estados Unidos nacieron todos en Virginia. Estos presidentes fueron George Washington, Thomas Jefferson, James Madison y James Monroe.

Thomas Jefferson

Living in Virginia

Every year people come to Virginia to go to music festivals. The Jumpin' Bluegrass Festival in Chesterfield County is one of the most famous music events in Virginia.

La vida en Virginia

Todos los años la gente visita Virginia para asistir a festivales de música. El festival *Jumpin' Bluegrass* del Condado de Chesterfield es uno de los eventos musicales más famosos de Virginia.

Miss Rhonda Vincent at a Bluegrass Festival in Virginia

Miss Rhonda Vincent en un festival de *bluegrass*, en Virginia

Many Virginians enjoy their beaches on the Atlantic Ocean. Virginia's beaches are good for swimming, fishing, and boating. They are also good for playing in the sand!

Muchos virginianos disfrutan de las playas del océano Atlántico. Las playas de Virginia son muy buenas para nadar, pescar y navegar. ¡También son muy buenas para jugar en la arena!

Virginia Beach, Virginia

At Colonial Williamsburg you can learn about Virginia's history and about Colonial America. At Colonial Williamsburg people dressed in old-fashioned clothes explain to visitors what life was like in the 1700s.

En Colonial Williamsburg puedes aprender acerca de la historia de Virginia y de la América colonial. En Colonial Williamsburg la gente, vestida con trajes de época, les explica a los visitantes cómo era la vida en el siglo XVIII.

Horse-drawn Carriage in Colonial Williamsburg

Carruaje de caballos en Colonial Williamsburg

Virginia Beach, Norfolk, Chesapeake, and Richmond are the biggest cities in Virginia. Richmond is the capital of the state of Virginia.

Virginia Beach, Norfolk, Chesapeake y Richmond son las ciudades más grandes de Virginia. Richmond es la capital del estado de Virginia.

Virgina State Capitol in Richmond

Capitolio del estado de Virginia en Richmond

Activity:
Let´s Draw the Map of Virginia

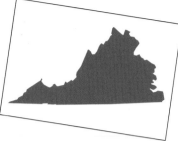

Actividad:
Dibujemos el mapa de Virginia

1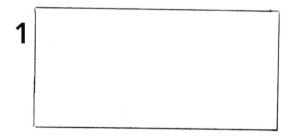

Begin with a rectangle.

Comienza con un rectángulo.

2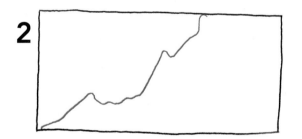

Add squiggly lines for the western border.

Agrega una línea quebrada para dibujar la frontera occidental.

3

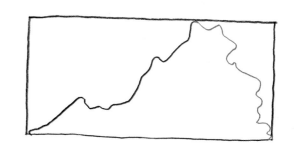

Next draw a squiggly line to make the eastern border.

Luego traza otra línea quebrada para dibujar la frontera oriental.

4

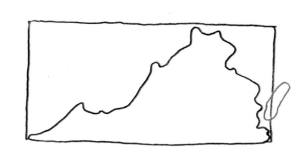

Add an island toward the lower right corner. This island is Delmarva.

Añade la isla Delmarva en la esquina inferior derecha.

5

Draw a star for Virginia's capital, Richmond. Erase the guidelines. Well done!

Dibuja una estrella en el lugar de Richmond, la capital. Borra las líneas de guía. ¡Muy bien!

Timeline   Cronología

1607 — The Jamestown Colony is founded. / Se funda la colonia Jamestown.

1781 — British surrender at Yorktown, ending the fighting in the American Revolution. / Los británicos se rinden en Yorktown, terminando así la lucha de la Revolución Americana.

1788 — Virginia becomes the tenth state to join the United States. / Virginia es el décimo estado en unirse a los Estados Unidos.

1819 — The University of Virginia is founded in Charlottesville by Thomas Jefferson. / Thomas Jefferson funda en Charlottesville la Universidad de Virginia.

1831 — Nat Turner, a slave, leads a slave uprising in Southampton. / El esclavo Nat Turner encabeza un levantamiento de esclavos en Southampton.

1865 — The Civil War ends at Appomattox Court House. / Termina la Guerra Civil en Appomattox Court House.

1989 — Douglas Wilder becomes Virginia's first African American governor. / Douglas Wilder llega a ser el primer gobernador afroamericano de Virginia.

Virginia Events	Eventos en Virginia
February	Febrero
George Washington Birthday Celebration, Alexandria	Celebración del cumpleaños de George Washington, en Alexandria
March	Marzo
St. Patrick's Day Parade, Alexandria	Desfile del Día de San Patricio, en Alexandria
June	Junio
Juneteenth Celebration, Alexandria	Celebración *Juneteenth,* en Alexandria
Potomac Celtic Festival, Leesburg	Festival celta de Potomac, en Leesburg
July	Julio
Virginia Scottish Games, Alexandria	Juegos escoceses de Virginia, en Alexandria
Bluegrass Live Festival, Middletown	Festival de *bluegrass,* en Middletown
August	Agosto
Cambodian Community Day, Alexandria	Día de la comunidad camboyana, en Alexandria
American Indian Festival, Alexandria	Festival indígena-americano, en Alexandria
September	Septiembre
American Music Festival, Virginia Beach	Festival de la música americana, en Virginia Beach
Italian Festival, Alexandria	Festival italiano, en Alexandria
Virginia State Fair, Richmond	Feria del estado de Virginia, en Richmond
October	Octubre
Virginia State Rose Show, Richmond	Exposición de la rosa del estado de Virginia, en Richmond
Fall Harvest Family Days, Mount Vernon	Días familiares de la cosecha de otoño, en Mount Vernon

Virginia Facts/Datos sobre Virginia

Population
7.3 million

Población
7.3 millones

Capital
Richmond

Capital
Richmond

State Motto
Sic Semper Tyrannis,
*Thus Always to
Tyrants*

Lema del estado
Así siempre a
los tiranos

State Flower
Dogwood

Flor del estado
Cornejo

State Bird
Cardinal

Ave del estado
Cardenal

State Nickname
Old Dominion State

Mote del estado
Estado del Antiguo Dominio

State Tree
Flowering dogwood

Árbol del estado
Cornejo

State Song
"Carry Me Back to
Old Virginia"

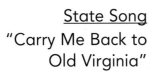

Canción del estado
"Llévenme de vuelta
a Virginia"

Famous Virginians/Virginianos famosos

Ella Fitzgerald
(1918–1996)

Singer

Cantante

George Washington
(1732–1739)

U.S. president

Presidente de E.U.A.

Thomas Jefferson
(1743–1826)

U.S. president

Presidente de E.U.A.

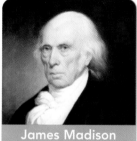

James Madison
(1751–1836)

U.S. president

Presidente de E.U.A.

Meriwether Lewis
(1774–1809)

Explorer

Explorador

William Clark
(1770–1838)

Explorer

Explorador

Words to Know/Palabras que debes saber

border

frontera

festival

festival

hilly

montañoso

old-fashioned

de época

Here are more books to read about Virginia:
Otros libros que puedes leer sobre Virginia:

In English/En inglés:

Virginia
by Jean F. Blashfield
Children's Press, 1999

Virginia History
by Karla Smith
Heinemann, 2002

Words in English: 324

Palabras en español: 357

Index

Índice